Rotherham Schools Loan Service
Maltby Library,
High Street, Maltby, Rotherham S66 8LD.

This book must be returned by the date specified at the time of issue as
the DUE DATE FOR RETURN

The loan may be extended (personally, by post, telephone or online) for
a further period, if the book is not required by another reader, by quoting
the barcode / author / title.

Enquiries: 01709 813034

www.rotherham.gov.uk/sls

D0417792

Published in Great Britain in 2010
by Caboodle Books Ltd

A Catalogue record for this book is available from the
British Library.

ISBN-13: 978-0-9562656-8-5

Typeset in Century by Paul Wilson

Printed and bound by CPI Group (UK) Ltd, Croydon, CR0 4YY

The paper and board used in the paperback by Caboodle Books Ltd
are natural recyclable products made from wood grown in sustain-
able forests. The manufacturing processes conform to the environ-
mental regulations of the country of origin.

Caboodle Books Ltd
Riversdale, 8 Rivock Avenue,
Steeton, BD20 6SA, U.K.
1535 656015
sabroad.com

CONTENTS

PREFACE

Towards the end of the nineteenth century large parts of the world were changing almost as rapidly as they are now. Lots of people were moving from the countryside to the towns and cities to work in the new factories. Others were leaving their native countries to settle in other parts of the world.

Some people realised that if they were not careful the stories that had been passed from generation to generation by word of mouth would be lost. So they travelled the world collecting and writing down folk tales, wonder stories and tales of cunning tricksters and publishing them.

In the last few decades a number of storytellers have taken these stories and begun to tell them again without reading from a book. Each teller uses a different style, and the way the stories are told changes from storyteller to storyteller.

These stories are some of the ones I tell, written as I tell them. Some I took from old collections and some I collected on the road myself, like *José's First Adventure*. I got this from a storyteller called Trudy Terry of Orange in Texas on the Louisiana border.

They are stories I enjoy telling. I hope you will enjoy reading them and hopefully you'll even pass them on to others so that they'll keep going round and round the world forever.

THE CLOAK OF NIGHT

Back when all the animals were given their coats and all the birds had been given their feathers, the celestial spinners took the last of the darkness and spun it into thread and the cosmic weavers took all that thread and wove it into the cloak of night.

Most of the animals and birds were happy with what they had been given. The lion loved its mane, the elephant was ecstatic about its trunk and the peacock could not stop looking at the reflection of its own tail.

Only one of them was unhappy and that was the raven. In those days the raven was the brightest bird in the world. Its feathers were all the colours of the rainbow, and a few others besides.

Wherever it went there were gasps of admiration and it was impossible for the raven not to be the centre of attention whether it wanted to be or not, and it certainly did not.

In truth the raven was incredibly shy, so one dark evening it took the cloak of night, wrapped it around its bright feathers and flew off to hide in the mountains.

Without the cloak of night the world stayed light for twenty four hours a day. Not only that, but the sun was always in the sky so the world got hotter, and hotter, and hotter.

All the animals and all the birds apart from the raven held a great council and it was decided that one of them should fly up to the cosmic weavers and ask them to weave a new cloak of night.

First the sparrow tried but she could not fly nearly high enough, then the lark who managed to get far higher but not high enough, finally the swallow tried and very soon it had soared further than the eye could see.

Eventually the swallow came to the looms of the cosmic weavers who were busy making a pattern of stars. To the swallow's surprise they were weaving them onto a light background.

She asked them if they would be kind enough to weave a new cloak of night but they simply pointed at their own work and with long faces told her that they had run out of dark thread long ago when they had first woven the cloak of night. Of course, if she could persuade the celestial spinners to spin some more black thread they would willingly make a new cloak for the night sky.

The swallow flew off to speak to the celestial spinners who were busy at their wheels spinning thread of silver and gold. She apologised for disturbing them and asked if they would be kind enough to spin enough black thread for the cosmic weavers to weave a new cloak of night.

They bowed their heads and said that they would be happy to spin enough black thread for a new cloak, but they had used all the darkness to spin the thread for the first cloak and now there was none left. They did assure her however, that if she could create some darkness they would do it straight away.

The swallow went back down to the world and told the animals and birds what the spinners and weavers had said.

They looked at each other, then up to the sky. Eventually, from the edge of the group came the timid voice of the doe.

"If only one of us could fly up and push the moon across the sun. That might create enough darkness for the spinners to work."

They all agreed that this was a fine plan and looked around for one of their number who was both strong enough to push the moon and who could fly high enough to reach it. All eyes fell upon the eagle but there was a problem: if the eagle pushed the moon with its beak the moon might burst. They needed someone to sit on the eagle's back to push the moon with their paws.

At first the lion volunteered but the eagle did not trust him at all. The eagle thought that when the job was done and they were nearly back on the ground the lion would eat him.

Then the elephant volunteered but even the eagle could not fly with the weight of an elephant on his back.

Finally the mouse put its hand up.

"I can do it," it squeaked.

All the animals laughed, but the eagle thought it was the best suggestion so far so the mouse clambered up onto the top of the eagle's head and off they flew. The pair soared higher, and higher, and higher until they came to the moon.

"Hold out your hands," ordered the eagle, "and push."

They pushed, and they pushed, and they pushed but it did not matter how hard they tried the moon would not budge.

"Hold tight!" cried the eagle. "I'll fly as hard as I can at the moon and you hold out your hands and we will see if that will move it."

The mouse gripped onto the eagle's head with its tiny back legs and wrapped its tail around the eagle's neck. The eagle flew as hard as it could at the moon and the mouse held out its hands. They crashed into the moon and to their delight the moon began to roll slowly towards the sun.

They did this over and over again, until gradually the moon rolled in front of the sun and blotted out all the light and there was nothing but darkness.

They kept rolling the moon on, and on, and on until once more the sun's rays shone down upon the earth because there has to be both light and darkness but in those few moments the celestial spinners managed to spin enough black thread for the cosmic weavers to weave a new cloak of night.

When the eagle and the mouse came back to earth a great feast had been prepared for them and it went on for a whole month with everyone congratulating them on their fine work.

However, ever since then, every so often, the mouse climbs on the head of the eagle and they fly off to roll the moon across the front of the sun so that the celestial spinners will always have a little darkness to work with and the cosmic weavers will always have a little spare black thread.

THE END

FISHY BUSINESS

One day Miko the fox, probably the most cunning creature in the world, was waiting in a snow hole by the side of the road for something to happen.

He did not know what was going to happen: he just knew it would be something and he knew that when it did he would have some fun, probably at someone else's expense.

Miko waited, and he waited, and he waited, but nothing happened.

So he waited, and he waited, and he waited, but *still* nothing happened.

So he waited, and he waited, and he waited, when all of a sudden he heard the sound of a reindeer bell in the distance.

The ringing got closer, and closer, and closer, until round the bend in the road Miko saw a reindeer dragging a sleigh, and driven by a reindeer man.

Behind the sleigh were five sledges. On each sledge were tied goods the reindeer man was taking to market.

The first sledge was full of furs, the second was full of wooden toys, the third was full of bags of kindling, the fourth was full of hats, coats and gloves and the fifth sledge was piled high with fish.

Miko thought for a second then threw himself in the road, becoming as stiff as a board so it seemed to all the world that he was dead.

When the reindeer man got closer he thought to himself what a good price he would get for a dead fox.

So he picked up Miko and put him on the first sledge. Then he shook his reins and the reindeer trotted on, pulling the sledges behind him.

He had hardly gone a few paces down the road when the reindeer man heard a thud.

He looked round and he saw the fox lying in the road.

So he picked the fox up, but this time he put him on the *second* sledge.

But the same thing happened again: the fox fell off the *second* sledge and when the reindeer man saw him lying on the road, he picked him up and put him on the *third* sledge.

This happened twice more until Miko was exactly where he wanted to be: on the *fifth* sledge full of fish.

As soon as the reindeer man was back on his sleigh Miko began chewing through the rope tying his sledge to the one in front.

Very soon he managed to gnaw right through the rope. So there he was sitting on top of a sledge full of fish in the middle of the road while the reindeer man, the reindeer and all the other sledges had disappeared over the horizon.

When the reindeer man got to the market he realised that the fish sledge was missing and went running back down the road to find it.

To his dismay all he found was an empty sledge. There was no sign of Miko or the fish.

The poor man hung his head and made his way back to the market.

Meanwhile Miko, who had carried the fish to a clearing in the forest, was feeling very pleased with himself.

Just then, who should come lumbering through the trees but his friend, Otso the bear.

Now in those days bears had big, bushy tails, and Otso the bear was very proud of his bushy tail, so as he walked he swung it from side just to show it off.

"Good afternoon Otso," chirped Miko. "Your tail is looking particularly magnificent today."

"Thank you very much," replied Otso, "and that is a fine catch you have there."

"Oh those," said Miko nonchalantly, "I caught all of them this morning and I must say it did not take me very long at all."

"Really!" exclaimed Otso. "How did you do that?"

"Simple!" said Miko. "I went down to the river, cut a hole in the ice, hung my tail through the hole and waited for the fish to hang onto my tail. When I had enough fish I stood up, picked the fish off my tail and put them in a basket. It was easy! Why don't you try?"

"I will," said Otso enthusiastically, and off he trotted swinging his tail behind him.

Miko smiled quietly to himself, picked out the largest of his fish and began to eat.

Down at the river Otso set about sawing a hole in the ice. When the hole was big enough he let his tail through into the icy water, sat down and waited.

He waited, and he waited, and he waited, but no fish bit at all.

So he waited, and he waited, and he waited, but *still* no fish bit.

So he waited, and he waited, and he waited, until he was so cold that he couldn't stand it any longer, and he tried to get up off the ice.

But poor Otso was completely stuck.

It didn't matter how much he wriggled and twisted, his tail was frozen into the ice.

So Otso pulled, and he pulled, and he pulled.

He pulled for so long, and he pulled so hard that eventually there was a loud 'pop' and he was free!

But when Otso tried to swing his tail, he realised it was missing!

He looked back to where he had been sitting, and there was his beautiful tail stuck in the ice.

Ever since then if you ever look at a bear, you will see that all they have is a very short stub of a tail.

And you will know that it was all the fault of Miko the fox, the most cunning creature in the world.

THE END

JACK AND HIS COMPANIONS

A long time ago, when all the animals could talk to each other and chickens still had teeth there was a boy called Jack who lived with his mother on a farm.

This year was a very bad year for the farm. The harvest was poor and there was almost nothing to eat.

So Jack decided to go and seek his fortune or at least live until the next harvest.

So he asked his mother for the little cake she was baking in the oven and a jug of milk to help him on his way.

His mother offered him half the cake, half a jug of milk and her best wishes. Jack thanked her, said goodbye and set off down the road.

He had hardly got around the first corner when he heard a stomping, and a clomping, and a braying from the stream below.

He looked down and he saw a donkey drowning in the stream.

As quickly as he could Jack got a pile of stones, built a bridge and pulled the donkey out.

"Thank you very much," said the donkey, "for I would have surely died and where do you happen to be going?"

"I'm off to seek my fortune", replied Jack, "or at least live until the next harvest."

"Do you mind if I come with you?" asked the donkey.

"Not at all," said Jack and they set off down the road together.

The two friends soon came to a city and as they walked towards the centre they caught sight of a group of children chasing a dog.

There was a kettle tied to the dog's tail and the children were throwing stones at the dog and throwing stones at the kettle.

Jack and the donkey hid behind a wall and waited for the group to pass by.

Just as they got level to them Jack shouted "Now!" and the donkey brayed as loud as it could.

The children were so frightened that they ran off in all directions. Jack caught the dog and untied the kettle from its tail.

"Thank you very much," said the dog, "for I would have surely died and where do you happen to be going?"

"We're off to seek our fortune" replied Jack, "or at least live until the next harvest."

"Do you mind if I come with you?" asked the dog.

"Not at all," said Jack and the donkey together, and they set off down the road.

By this time they were getting quite hungry so they all sat down by the side of the road for something to eat.

The dog found a bone, the donkey found some thistles and Jack ate his cake.

They had hardly swallowed their first few mouthful when along came a cat that was so thin it could have hidden behind a pencil.

"It looks like you have seen nine rooftops since breakfast," said Jack. "Would you like a saucer of milk?"

The cat lapped up the saucer of milk and you know exactly what it said:

"Thank you very much, for I would have surely died and where do happen to be going?"

"We're off to seek our fortune," replied Jack, "or at least live until the next harvest."

"Do you mind if I come with you?" asked the cat.

"Not at all," chorused Jack, the donkey and the dog and they set off down the road.

As the four friends rounded a bend in the road they saw, running in front of them, a fox and in the fox's mouth was a cockerel.

"Quick after him!" said Jack and the dog gave chase to the fox.

The fox was fast but the dog was faster still and as caught up to the fox, the fox dropped the cockerel.

The cockerel got on the dog's back and they went back to Jack and as if you didn't know it, this is what the cockerel said:

"Thank you very much, for I would have surely died and where do you happen to be going?"

"We're off to seek our fortune," replied Jack, "or at least live until the next harvest."

"Do you mind if I come with you?" asked the cockerel.

"Not at all," said Jack, the donkey, the dog and the cat and they set off down the road.

At this point it was getting dark so they started looking for somewhere to sleep.

Unfortunately, there was no cottage in sight so they all lay down to sleep in a clearing in the woods.

All except the cockerel, who went to sleep on the branch of a tree.

They had only been asleep for a few moments when the cockerel started crowing.

"What's all that noise?" complained the donkey.

"It must be morning," said the cockerel. "There is a light over there, it must be the sun rising."

"Don't be silly," said the donkey. "That's not the sun, that's a candle in a cottage window. It wasn't there earlier - we had better wake up Jack and the others and find out what is going on."

So Jack, the donkey, the dog, the cat and the cockerel crept down to the cottage and peered in through the window and there inside were six robbers. One was eating chicken legs, one was drinking from a big tankard and one was counting gold and silver.

"When I give the signal," said Jack, "make as much noise as you can."

Jack held up his hand and counted: "One, two, three," and the donkey started braying, the dog started barking, the cat started meowing and the cockerel started crowing.

When they heard all the noise the robbers were so frightened that they ran out of the back door of the cottage and went and hid in the woods.

So Jack and his companions went inside the cottage and made themselves comfortable.

The dog settled down by the fire, the cat curled up on the table in the kitchen, the cockerel perched on top of the door, the donkey made herself comfortable in the stable and Jack lay down in bed ready for a good night's sleep.

Meanwhile in the woods the robbers were complaining.

"I'd hardly had a bite from my chicken," said one.

"I'd hardly put my tankard to my lips," said another.

"Think of all that gold and silver," said a third.

The robber chief couldn't stand their whining a second longer.

"Alright," he said, "I'll go down the cottage and find out what is going on."

So the robber chief crept down to the cottage, pushed open the door and tiptoed inside.

It was so dark he couldn't see his finger in front of his nose.

As he got to the fireplace he tripped over the dog and the dog bit him all up his legs.

So he ran into the kitchen but he was set upon by the cat who scratched him all down his front

Then he ran out of the door but the cockerel dropped down from the top of the door and pecked him all over his face.

Desperate to get away he ran to the stable where he met the donkey who kicked him so hard he flew all the way back to the woods.

"Whatever happened to you?" asked the other robbers when they saw that his clothes had been torn and that he was covered in scratches.

"Well it's like this: I went down to the cottage and I crept inside and it was so dark I couldn't see my finger in front of my nose!

"The first thing I did was creep over to the fireplace but I tripped over an old woman brushing out the wool with a wire brush, getting it ready to spin. She got that wire brush and stuck it into my legs!

"So I ran into the kitchen and there was a cobbler mending shoes and he got his needle and scratched me all over my front!

"Then I ran out of the door but a little man dropped down from the top of the door with a three pronged fork and he stuck it right in my face!

"So I ran to the stable and there was a man with a big hammer who hit me so hard I flew all the way back to the woods!

"We had better leave this place and never go near that cottage again."

And so that's what they did.

But we know what really happened to the robber chief, don't we?

As for Jack and his companions they found out where all the things in the cottage had been stolen from and they gave them all back to their owners, who rewarded the friends so handsomely they lived in the cottage in luxury for the rest of their lives.

As for you, if any of you happen to be passing by Jack's cottage and knock on the door you will be made welcome by Jack, the donkey, the dog, the cat and the cockerel. You are sure to be given something tasty to eat, something thirst quenching to drink and if you are very tired a comfortable bed to sleep in.

THE END

KATE CRACKERNUTS

Way back in time when mountains were taller, rivers were deeper and forests were thicker, there lived a king with his daughter, a beautiful princess.

The queen had died some time ago and the king decided that it was time to marry again. So he found a new queen who had a daughter who was exactly the same age as the princess and whose name was Kate.

Kate and the princess soon became great friends but the queen was not so happy.

The queen was worried that the whole kingdom thought the princess was more beautiful than her daughter Kate, and so she decided to do something about it.

So the queen climbed to the top of the hill where the hen wife lived and knocked on her door.

"Yes?" asked the hen wife, "can I help you?"

"Everyone in the kingdom thinks the princess is more beautiful than my daughter Kate and I want you to think of something to change their minds," replied the queen.

"Easy," said the hen wife. "Tomorrow morning send her up to collect six eggs for the king's breakfast. But make sure that she has nothing to eat before she comes."

The next day the princess got up early to climb the hill to the hen wife's hut. But as she passed through the palace kitchen she spied the maid spreading jam on fresh toast and her mouth started watering.

She asked the maid if she could have a small corner of toast, and of course the maid agreed. As she ate it she went out through the rose garden and through the vegetable garden where the gardener's boy was collecting peas.

She wiped the jam from the corner of her mouth and walked up the hill. When she reached the top of the hill she tapped lightly on the hen wife's door.

"Yes, can I do something for you?" asked the hen wife.

The princess asked for six eggs for the king's breakfast. She was instructed to go to the table and unscrew the lid on the jar of eggs that rested in the middle of the table. Once the lid was off she was to take out the eggs.

She did just as the hen wife told her. But when nothing happened the hen wife knew she must have had something to eat before she had come.

"Tell the queen to make sure the pantry door is locked," said the hen wife as the princess left with the eggs.

When the queen heard the message she pretended not to be angry. But the next day she walked with the princess through the kitchen and out into the rose garden just to make sure she did not eat any of the maid's breakfast.

The princess then went into the vegetable garden where the gardener's boy was collecting peas.

She asked the boy for a few pods and popped the peas out of their pods and into her mouth as she climbed the hill towards the hen wife's hut, throwing the empty pods over her shoulder as she went.

She knocked on the hen wife's door a second time and once more she asked for six eggs for the king's breakfast but the same thing happened as before.

The next morning the queen walked with the princess through the kitchen, through the rose garden, through the vegetable garden where the gardener's boy was collecting peas, and half way up the hill, so by the time the princess came to the hen wife's door she had had nothing to eat at all.

Again she asked for six eggs for the king's breakfast and again she was told to unscrew the lid of the jar on the table and take the eggs.

However this time as she lifted the lid a sheep's head jumped out of the jar and onto her shoulders and her own head jumped off her shoulders and into the jar.

The princess screamed, ran out of the hut, hid behind a hedge near the palace and covered her head with a shawl so nobody could see her.

Meanwhile back at the palace Kate began to wonder where her best friend was.

She looked behind one hedge and she wasn't there, she looked behind another and she wasn't there either but when she looked behind a third hedge she found the princess crying sorrowfully.

"Kate, I've got a sheep's head on my shoulders," whimpered the princess.

Now Kate was exactly the kind of friend you would want in a crisis, because she didn't get worried about anything.

"Well if you've got a sheep's head on your shoulders," said Kate in a matter of fact kind of way, "we need find a way to break the spell. Come with me and we will find an answer."

The two girls travelled for a long way and further still, till their feet were sore and their throats were dry.

Just as they were about to collapse from exhaustion they spied a castle in the distance.

Kate banged on the big oak front door of the castle and it was opened by an old servant.

"Do you have somewhere for us to stay tonight?" pleaded Kate. "My sister is very ill."

"Upstairs is a very unwell prince," replied the servant. "If you are prepared to watch over him tonight you may stay."

Kate thanked the servant, and the two girls were shown upstairs to the prince's room.

The prince was on one side of the room, fast asleep, the princess was on the other with a sheep's head on her shoulders, and Kate was in the middle making up the fire.

At midnight Kate saw the prince get out of bed and walk round the room, and down the stairs and towards the stables. Kate followed him every step of the way.

When he got to the stables he saddled up his favourite horse and climbed on its back, and Kate got on behind him.

They rode through the forest. As they were riding Kate took hazelnuts from one tree and hazelnuts from another and put them in her apron. They rode until they came to green hill and the prince shouted, "Open up, open up, for it is a prince and his horse."

No sooner were the words out of his mouth than the green hill opened and they rode inside. Kate realised at once that she was in the land of the fairies so she found a hiding place in the shadows. As two dancers passed by she listened to what they were saying.

"If only Kate knew if she could get the stick off the baby and touch the princess on the head three times with she would have own head back."

When Kate heard these words she took some hazelnuts from her pocket and rolled them across the floor in front of the baby. The baby dropped the stick and crawled across the floor towards the nuts. Kate grabbed the stick and put it in her apron and all this time the baby did not cry once.

When it was time to go she got on the back of the horse behind the prince and rode back through the forest. The prince put the horse back in the stables, walked back up the stairs into his room and went back to bed.

Kate took the stick and touched the princess on the head three times and believe it or not, she immediately had her own head back.

The next morning the king came to visit his son, bringing with him the court doctor, a miserable man if ever there was one.

"How is my boy this morning?" asked the king.

"He is no better," replied the doctor.

"At least he is not any worse. Thank you young lady for looking after him," said the king. "What, may I ask is your name?"

At that moment Kate had a mouth full of hazelnuts and when she answered "Kate, Your Majesty" she sprayed tiny pieces of nut across the whole room.

"Kate Crackernuts most likely," sniffed the doctor.

"Maybe so," said the king, "but I am very grateful to you for looking after my son. Would you do me the service of looking after him for one more night?"

Of course Kate and the princess agreed.

Despite having her own head back the princess was very tired so that night she slept just as she had the night before. The prince also slept as he had the night before, and just as *she* had the night before Kate sat in the middle making up the fire.

At midnight the prince rose from his bed again, went to the stables, got on his horse and rode through the forest to the green hill. Kate, just as she had the previous night, rode on the horse behind him.

The prince shouted for the hill to open and once inside Kate found her hiding place in the shadows.

Again two dancers passed by and again she listened to their words. "If only Kate knew, if she could only get the dead bird from the baby who is playing with it in the corner and get the prince to have three mouthfuls of it, the prince would be completely cured."

It is one thing to get a stick from a baby but a bird is a different matter, and it took three handfuls of nuts rolling across the floor before the baby dropped the bird and crawled after the nuts. Kate grabbed the bird and put it in her apron and all this time the baby did not cry once.

When it was time to go they rode through the forest, put the horse back in the stables and went back to the prince's room where the prince got back into bed and continued snoring like nothing had happened.

Kate plucked the bird's feathers, put the bird on the end of a stick and started roasting it on the fire.

Now the prince was one of those people who doesn't have to be awake to be hungry and when the smell of the bird cooking reached his nostrils he put out a hand to try a piece.

No sooner was it in his hand than he put it in his mouth and put his hand out for second piece.

When the prince's hand stretched out for third time Kate took the whole bird and put it in his hand, and he put the whole bird in his mouth and spat out the bones but by this time he had swallowed his three mouthfuls and he was totally cured.

The prince began bouncing off his bed, bouncing off the ceiling and bouncing off the four walls.

His father, the king, came running up the stairs to see what all the noise was about.

When he realised that his son was cured he was so pleased he offered Kate his son's hand in marriage and he offered the princess the prince's younger brother's hand in marriage. And then there was a great wedding and a great feast which I believe is going on to this very day. So if you find it, invite yourself in and eat till you are completely satisfied.

THE END

MOSSYCOAT

Way back in time, when mountains were taller and forests were thicker and rivers were deeper there lived a girl called Mossycoat, who was the most beautiful girl in the village.

All the young men wanted to marry Mossycoat, especially the local tinker - the man that went from door to door selling and mending pots and pans.

Every day he would bring her presents: sometimes a necklace, sometimes a bracelet and sometimes ear rings.

She loved the presents but she did not want to marry the man.

Mossycoat went to her mother and told her the problem.

"Do not worry," said her mother, "for I am making this petticoat. When it is finished all our troubles will be over."

"In the meantime tell him he cannot marry you unless he brings you a dress of white satin with gold leaves on it the size of a man's hand - and it must fit *perfectly*."

Mossycoat ran down the stairs to where the tinker was waiting and told him her mother had said she could not marry him unless he brought her a dress of white satin with gold leaves on it the size of a man's hand - and it had to fit *perfectly*.

The tinker took her measurements and off he went. A week later he was back with the dress - and it fitted *perfectly*.

Mossycoat ran back to her mother and told her what had happened.

"Do not worry," she said, "for I have nearly finished the petticoat."

"In the meantime tell him you cannot marry him unless he brings you a dress of silk the colours of the birds of the sky - and it must fit *perfectly*."

Again she told him what her mother had said except for the part about the petticoat and again he went off to fetch the dress and again he returned with the very thing - and again it fitted *perfectly*.

Once more Mossycoat ran back to her mother and told her what had happened.

"Do not worry," said her mother for the third time, "for I have nearly finished the petticoat."

"In the meantime tell him you cannot marry him unless he brings you a pair of silver slippers and they must be neither too big nor too small - they must fit *perfectly*."

When Mossycoat told the tinker this he looked at her feet, which were only three inches long, and off he went.

A week later he was back and what did he have, but a pair of silver slippers. They were neither too big nor too small - they fitted *perfectly*.

By this time Mossycoat was desperate but her mother, as always, remained calm.

"Do not worry," she whispered, "for I have nearly finished the petticoat."

"In the meantime tell him if he meets you outside the church at ten o'clock tomorrow morning you will be married."

Her mother had been right so far but Mossycoat was now more than a little worried.

"My mother says," stammered Mossycoat, "that if you meet me outside the church at ten o'clock tomorrow morning we will be married."

Well, the tinker was very happy when he heard this and he started laughing and doing cartwheels down the street. Meanwhile Mossycoat ran back to her mother.

"Mother what have you done to me?"

"Do not worry," said her mother, as calm as always, "for I have finished the petticoat."

And it was not any ordinary petticoat but a petticoat of moss with gold threads running through it. The petticoat was magical and it would take Mossycoat anywhere she wanted to go.

Her mother, who knew a thing or two about the future, told her to put on her mossy petticoat, and over the top of it she was to put on her dirtiest, shabbiest working clothes.

She was then to take her best clothes, put them in a bundle under her arm and wish herself one hundred miles away. When she got there she was to walk till she came to big house. She was to knock on the front door and ask for a job.

Well Mossycoat, as we know, was an obedient daughter, so she did everything her mother said.

When Mossycoat knocked on the door of the big house it was opened by the mistress herself, who asked her what she wanted. When Mossycoat asked for a job the mistress wanted to know what exactly she could do.

"I am the best cook in the world," said Mossycoat with an air of confidence that surprised even her.

"I have already got a cook," said the mistress, "but you can be the undercook - the cook's assistant," and she took her downstairs and introduced her to all the other servants.

Now, in those days the best job in the kitchen was to be the cook, and the second best was to be the undercook.

The other servants were certainly not going to let this little travelling girl take the second best job in the kitchen, so as soon as the mistress was out of the way they gave her all the really nasty jobs to do, like sweeping out the fireplace and cleaning the grease off the pans.

They would not even let her wash at the end of her work, so Mossycoat soon had dirt from the tip of her toes to the tip of her nose.

Well, life carried on like this for quite some time. But one day news came of a great dance that was to last for three whole nights.

On the afternoon of the first night of the dance the mistress called Mossycoat to her room. All the other servants thought she was going to lose her job but to Mossycoat's surprise the mistress invited her to the dance with herself, the master and their son.

"Thank you kindly ma'am," replied Mossycoat, "but look at me. If I sat in your fine carriage I would make the seats all greasy and dirty and if any fine gentleman sat next to me I would make his fine suit all stained and disgusting. Thank you kindly ma'am but I can't."

She curtsied politely and went back downstairs to the servants' quarters. When they asked what the mistress had wanted she told them she had been invited to the dance.

"You are a liar!" they shouted and hit her on the head with skillets, which are big cast iron frying pans.

The next day the same thing happened again, again she was called a liar and again she was hit on the head with skillets. But this time she was a little upset, so she used a magic enchantment to put all the servants to sleep.

She then went to her room, put on her mossy petticoat, her silver slippers and her dress of white satin with gold leaves on it the size of a man's hand and wished herself to the dance.

Mossycoat danced all night and had a wonderful time. But whenever she was asked where she came from all she would say was that she came from a place where they hit her on the head with skillets.

At the end of the night she made her excuses, went out into the corridor and wished herself back to the big house. The next morning she woke up all the other servants.

"Whatever happened to us?" they asked.

"You have been asleep," she replied.

"Please don't tell the mistress," they begged and they gave her soap, stockings and their week's money to keep quiet.

Well, the servants were kind to Mossycoat for a few minutes, but the next day when the same thing happened again, again she was called a liar and again she was hit on the head with skillets.

So once more she put the servants to sleep and went to her room.

This time she put on her mossy petticoat, her silver slippers and her dress of silk, the colours of the birds of the sky.

When she was dressed she wished herself back to the dance and danced all night with the mistress's son.

Whenever the young man asked her where she was from he got the same answer: she was from a place where they hit her on the head with skillets.

At the end of the night she tried to get away but the mistress's son was one of those boys who holds on far too tight, so she just wished herself away from within his embrace.

As she flew away his hand must have just touched her foot, because one silver slipper fell off and was left behind.

Back at the big house once more she woke up the servants and once more they gave her presents so she would not tell the mistress, but the mistress's son could not sleep.

"Mum I am in love! Mum I have to find her! Mum I cannot stand it!" he exclaimed.

"Neither can I," replied his mother, "and if it will keep you quiet we will get all the girls of the land and try the silver slipper on each of them, so we will know who she was."

So all of the girls in the land came to try on the slipper, but it fitted none of them. The only one who had not tried it on was Mossycoat. As soon as she tried it on it fitted *perfectly*.

He was about take her in his arms when she held up her hand.

"Wait a moment," she said, and went to her room. When she came back she was wearing the dress of white satin with gold leaves on it the size of a man's hand.

He was about to take her in his arms again when *again* she held up her hand.

"Wait a moment," she said, and once more she went to her room. This time she returned wearing the dress of silk the colours of the birds of the sky.

This time he had learned his lesson and he asked her to tell him her story. So Mossycoat told him those parts she wanted him to hear but she said nothing about being hit on the head with skillets.

"The one thing I don't understand," he said, "was that you came from a place where they hit you on the head with skillets."

Mossycoat said not a single word, but just looked round at all the other servants.

The master and the mistress and their son then understood perfectly and the servants were driven from the house by the master's dogs.

New servants were soon found for the house, and then they held a great wedding with all kinds of fine food and drink.

And if you had been there then of course you would have been invited.

THE END

THE GOLDEN RAM

Way back in time, beyond the seven hills and the seven rivers there lived a hunter with his wife and young son.

Every day he would go out into the forest and bring back food for his family: sometimes a pheasant, sometimes a rabbit and sometimes, if they were very lucky, a deer.

One day the hunter was out in the forest when out from between the trees came a golden ram - a male sheep.

The hunter was about to put his gun to his shoulder and shoot it when the ram charged him, knocked him down and killed him.

He lay where he fell for a week until his neighbours found him. They carried his body home and his wife buried it, then she took the gun and hung it over the fireplace.

She turned to their young son and said, "Whatever you do, do not touch the gun."

But you know what it is like if you are told not to do something: you just have to do it. So as soon

45

as he grew tall enough to reach the gun he stretched up and took the gun down from above the fireplace. He then went out into the forest, and he was not there for long before out from between the trees came the golden ram.

"I killed your father and I shall kill you," snorted the ram.

"I think not," replied the boy and, putting his gun to his shoulder, he shot the ram between the eyes. He took out his knife, cut off the golden fleece and returned home.

The news of the golden fleece spread far and wide and soon the king got to hear of it.

The king told the boy to bring it to him because he wanted to see what wonderful beasts were living in his forest. When he saw it of course he wanted it and he asked the boy how much he would sell it for.

"I can't sell you this," replied the boy, "for it is the fleece of the ram that killed my father."

Now the king was satisfied with this answer, if a little taken aback, but the king had a chief adviser who also happened to be the boy's uncle. The uncle was no friend of the boy but his mortal enemy.

"Well if he won't sell it to you then set him a task. If he cannot complete that task in seven days then cut off his head," advised the wicked uncle.

"Very well," said the king. "You have seven days to grow me a vineyard. On the seventh day bring me a bunch of grapes and set it at my feet: if not I will cut off your head."

The boy ran home to his mother in a panic and told her everything the king had said.

"I told you not to touch your father's gun," was all his mother had to say before turning her back on him and carrying on with her work.

Getting no sympathy at home he went out into the forest, sat on a log with his head in his hands and cried. All he could think about was how long he was going to be able to keep his head on shoulders.

After he had been there for some time a beautiful girl appeared from between the trees. He did not want to look like he had been crying so he wiped his eyes and asked her who she was.

"I am the maid of the woods," she said, "and you are in trouble."

"I know I am in trouble," replied the boy, and he told her the whole story.

"Do not worry about it," she said. "What you must do is this: go to the king, ask him where he wants his vineyard planted, lay down in that place with your arms crossed and a sprig of basil on your chest and go to sleep. When you wake up the vineyard will be growing around you. On the seventh day take a bunch of grapes and lay them at the feet of the king."

The boy ran home and told his mother exactly what the girl had said.

"You might as well do it," said the mother. "You are going to have your head cut off anyway."

Taking notice of both his mother and the girl he went back to the king and did everything the girl had said. On the seventh day he was able to take a bunch of grapes and lay them at the king's feet.

"Obviously that was far too easy," complained the wicked uncle. "Set him something else to do. If he cannot do that in seven days then cut off his head."

"Very well," replied the king. "Boy, you have seven days to build me a palace of elephant tusks: if not I will cut off your head."

The boy ran home once more and told his mother what had happened.

"Go to the forest and see your girlfriend," was all his mother had to say. So off went the boy to the forest once again. And again the beautiful girl appeared before him.

"You are in trouble again," she said.

"I know I'm in trouble," said the boy and once more he told the girl the whole story.

"Do not worry," she said. "Go to the king. Ask him for two ships, twenty five of his finest carpenters and three hundred barrels of the strongest sleeping draught he has.

"Sail to a place where the mountains meet at the sea and the river flows in between, dam the river and pour the sleeping draught in the lake behind the dam.

"The elephants will come down at night, drink from the lake and fall fast asleep.

"While they are asleep tell the carpenters to cut off their tusks, load them onto the ships and take them to where the king wants his palace built.

"You may then go to sleep. When you wake up the palace will be built around you."

The boy followed the girls instructions and everything happened exactly as she said.

"The boy must be a sorcerer," sneered the wicked uncle. "Give him one more job to do. If he does it cut off his head anyway."

"Very well," said the king. "Boy - in such and such a land lives a princess. Bring her to me: if not you know exactly what will happen to you."

The boy went and told his mother who sent him to the forest once more to see the girl.

No sooner had the boy sat down on the tree trunk than the girl appeared.

"You are in trouble again," she said. "Can't you stay out of trouble for two minutes?"

"I know I'm in trouble!" exclaimed the boy. "Will you stop telling me I'm in trouble? I've got to go to such and such a land but I don't even know where the land is! I have got to bring back a princess but I don't even know what she looks like! And you tell me I am in trouble? Of course I am in trouble!"

"Do not worry," she said, "but listen carefully because this is the complicated part. Go to the king and ask him for a galley - a big ship. Divide that galley into twelve shops and fill each shop with the finest of goods, silks, perfumes and jewels. Have handsome young man serving in each shop. When you have all this set sail. On the voyage you will meet a man with an eagle. Pay him whatever he asks for the eagle, take a feather from the eagle's tail and set the eagle free.

"Next you will meet a man with a golden carp - a big goldfish. Pay him whatever he asks for the golden carp, take a scale from the back of the golden carp and set the carp free.

"Finally you will meet a man with a dove. Pay him whatever he asks for the dove, take a feather from the wing of the dove and set the dove free.

"Eventually you will reach such and such a land. The people of that land will see your fine goods, news will reach the princess and she will come down with her ladies in waiting. When she reaches the seventh shop you must set sail, and when she reaches the twelfth shop she will realise she is in the middle of the ocean.

"The princess will not be happy and she will take a bird from her shoulder, write a note to her father, tie it to the bird's leg and send it to him. When this happens take the eagle's feather and burn it. The eagle will catch the bird and it will not reach her father. When she realises this she will take a small pebble and throw it over the side of the ship and the ship will be stilled, it will not move. When this happens take the scale of the golden carp and burn it.

"The carp will swallow the pebble and the ship will continue on its voyage. When the princess realises this she will stop the galley for a second time and tell you that she will not allow it to move until she has in her possession some of the elixir - the liquid of life.

"When this happens, take the dove's feather and burn it. The dove will come to you and you will put a flask in the dove's beak. The dove will fly away and when it returns the flask will be full. You may then go home."

Well, you may believe it or not as you like but everything happened exactly as the girl said.

When the galley arrived back in port, the first person to get off was the princess, followed by her ladies in waiting. Next were the twelve handsome young men and last of all was the boy himself. As he stepped off the king shouted, "Seize him! Off with his head!"

And there he was, head to one side, body to the other.

Now as it happened the princess had become quite fond of the boy in the course of their journey so she asked the king where the boy was who had brought her across the ocean.

"There he is," said the king, "head to one side, body to the other."

The princess bent down, and gently picking up the boy's head she put it back on his shoulders. She then got some of the elixir of life and put some on his eyes, some on his lips and some on the cut on his neck. He was as good as new. You could not even see the join.

Now, it is said that anyone who was dead and has come alive again knows all things. This is not something to try but the king was one of those people who always wanted things he didn't have, so he ordered his own head to be cut off too.

"I am not sure this is such a good idea your majesty," suggested one advisor after another but the king refused to listen.

"If I say cut off my head, then I mean cut off my head."

"Very well your majesty," they said, and with that they cut off the king's head.

"Alright girl," they said to the princess. "Bring him back to life."

"You must be joking," she said and with that she pulled out a quill pen and wrote a message to her father saying she wished to marry the young man.

Her father sent a message back saying he would only give her his blessing if the people of that land elected her to be queen and the boy to be king.

So that is exactly what they did and there was a great wedding and a great coronation and had you been there you would have been invited too.

THE END

THE THREE GOLDEN HAIRS
OF
GRANDFATHER ALL KNOW

A long time ago beyond the seven hills and the seven rivers there lived a king and to tell you the truth he was not a very clever king.

One day when he was hunting in the forest he got separated from his companions and he became completely lost. As night drew in he caught sight of a light between the trees. He pushed his way through the undergrowth and found a dilapidated cottage, and when he knocked on the door it was opened by a charcoal burner. Now the charcoal burner was the poorest man in all the land.

"Show me the way back to my palace," demanded the king without so much as a "Good evening."

"I would love to your majesty," replied the charcoal burner, "but my wife is very ill and she is expecting a baby this very night. Please make yourself comfortable on the clean straw upstairs and I will show you the way back in the morning."

The king was not very happy about this but there was nothing he could do, and besides he was very tired, so he went upstairs, curled up on the clean straw and was soon fast asleep.

He had only just fallen asleep when he woke up again to the sound of howling and wailing downstairs. He peered through the floor boards and there below was the charcoal burner with a newborn baby boy in his arms. Sitting next to him were three witches.

The first witch took the boy in her arms and said, "I give this boy the gift of great dangers."

The second witch took the boy in her arms and said "I give this boy the gift of escaping from those great dangers."

The third took the boy in her arms and said, "I give this boy the gift of marrying the new born daughter of that king sleeping upstairs."

"What?" thought the king, "the queen has given birth to a daughter while I have been away and she is going to marry the son of the poorest man in all of the land. Impossible!"

When the king came down the next day he looked at the child and told the charcoal burner that a broken-down cottage was no place to bring up a baby boy and that he should send him to the palace to be looked after by the servants. Not only that, but the charcoal burner would be given a bag of gold.

The charcoal burner was not at all happy to give up his son to be cared for by the king's servants but it was difficult to turn down such a reasonable request by the king so he agreed.

When the king got back to the palace he called his most trusted servant, gave him a bag of gold and told him to give it to the charcoal burner in exchange for a baby. On the way home the servant was to throw the baby in the river and let him drown - if not he would be tasting water himself.

The servant did exactly as the king commanded. He gave the charcoal burner the bag of gold, the charcoal burner gave him a baby in a basket and on the way home the servant dropped the basket and the baby into the river from a high bridge. He told the king he had followed his instructions to the letter. But as it happened, the basket landed the right way up in the water and floated away.

The basket floated down to the estuary where there was a fisherman pulling in his nets. In one of his nets was the basket and in the basket was the baby. The baby was as happy as could be and no harm had come to him. The fisherman, having no children of his own, decided to bring him up like he was his own son.

Years later, the king was riding through his kingdom, when he came upon the fisherman and the boy.

"Why fisherman, that is a fine lad you have there. Is he yours?"

"Not exactly," replied the fisherman, "for eighteen years ago to this very day I found him floating down the river in a basket and having no children of my own I brought him up as if he was my own son."

The king realized at once that this was the charcoal burner's son so he told the fisherman that such a fine young lad could do no better than apply to be a guard at the palace and that he would write a letter of introduction to the queen himself.

The boy thought this a great opportunity, so he thanked the fisherman for all the kindness he had shown and gratefully accepted the king's offer. The king took a sheet of parchment and a quill pen and wrote:

Dear Queen,
This boy is my mortal enemy, when he gets to the
palace cut off his head immediately.
Yours truly
The King

He rolled the parchment up, put the king's seal on it and gave it to the boy who, thinking he had a letter of introduction, put it in his pocket and set off to the palace.

Luckily it took longer than a day to reach the palace. On the first night he came to a hut, knocked on the door and it was opened by the *second* witch.

"Come in," she said.

"I will," he said.

"Sit down," she said.

"I will," he said.

"Lay down," she said.

"I will," he said.

"Go to sleep," she said and before he could reply he was snoring his head off.

She put her hand in his pocket, pulled out the letter and read it.

"Impossible," she thought, and taking her hand she wiped it over the letter and made all the words fall off. Taking a quill pen, she wrote in the king's own handwriting:

Dear Queen,
This young man is the finest boy I have ever met in my life, when he gets to the palace tell him to marry my daughter immediately.
Yours truly
The King

The witch sealed the letter and put it back in the boy's pocket.

The next morning the boy continued on his journey. When he came to the palace he was taken to the queen. Well, you should have seen the surprise on her face when she read the letter. But she decided that if that was what the king wanted then that was what should happen.

By the time the king returned to the palace the deed was done and the charcoal burner's son was married to his daughter. The king was furious.

"Well, if you are married to my daughter there is little I can do about it. But you must fetch me a present: bring me three golden hairs from the head of Grandfather All Know."

"If that's what you want then that's what I'll get," said the boy and he set off on his journey.

The first place he came to was the river where there was a ferryman rowing passengers across. As he ferried the boy over the water he asked him where he was going.

"I'm off to Grandfather All Know," replied the boy.

"I'm glad you are going to see Grandfather All Know," said the ferryman, "for I have been stuck on this ferryboat for five years. Can you ask him how I can get off?"

The boy said he would and travelled on till he came to a city. The people of that city took him to their king.

"I'm glad you're going to see Grandfather All Know," said the king, "for in this city used to flow a stream and if you were very ill and very near death, you could drink from that stream and you would be well again. But that stream hasn't flowed for five years. Can you ask him how we can get the stream flowing again?"

Again the boy agreed and travelled on to the next city where he was again taken to their king.

"I'm glad you are going to see Grandfather All Know," said the king, "for in this city grows a tree and that tree used to bear fruit and if you were very old and very near death you could eat of that fruit and you would be be well again. But that tree hasn't borne fruit for five years. Would you ask him how we can get the fruit back on the tree?"

Once more the boy agreed. This time he journeyed on until he came to a hut, and it was the hut of the *third* witch. She asked him his business and he told her he was looking for Grandfather All

Know. He also told her about needing the three golden hairs and the answers to the three questions.

"You have come to the right place," she said. "For I am the mother of Grandfather All Know and Grandfather All Know is the sun. In the morning he is a baby, at midday he is a young man and in the evening he is an old, old man. He'll eat anybody and he'll eat you, so you had better hide under the trough."

That night in came Grandfather All Know sniffing the air and complaining that he could smell humans but as far as he could see there were none to eat.

"Never mind that," said his mother. "Put your head on my lap and go to sleep."

As soon as he was asleep she pulled out one of the golden hairs and threw it on the ground.

"Mother I am trying to get some sleep," grumbled Grandfather All Know.

"I am sorry," she said, "but I was having a dream and in the dream was a tree and that tree used to bear fruit and if you were very old and very near death you could eat of that fruit you would be young again. But that tree hasn't born any fruit for five years and I cannot get back to sleep until I have found a way to get the fruit back on the tree."

"Easy," replied the old man. "All you have to do is dig up the tree, unwrap the snake from around the roots and let it go and the fruit will be back by the morning."

"Thank you, now go back to sleep."

Hardly was he back to sleep when his mother pulled out a second hair and dropped it on the floor.

"Mother I am trying to get some sleep!" shouted Grandfather All Know.

"I'm sorry but I was having this dream," explained his mother. "I dreamt I was in a city and there used to be stream running through that city and if you were very ill and very near death you could drink from the stream and you would be well again. But that stream hasn't flowed for five years and I can't get back to sleep until I finish the dream and get it flowing again."

"Easy. Go to the spring which is the stream's source, put your hand down the hole, pull out the toad that is blocking it and the stream will start flowing straight away."

"Thank you, now go back to sleep."

He had not even let out his first snore before his mother pulled out the third hair and let it fall to the floor.

"Mother, I have a full day's work tomorrow, let me get some sleep."

"I'm sorry," she said, "but I was having another dream. I dreamt that there was a ferryman rowing people from one side of the river to the other and he had been stuck on that ferry for five years and I can't get back to sleep until I can finish the dream and get the ferryman off of that ferry."

"Easy. All he has to do is wait till he has a passenger, row them to the other side of the river, pass them the oar and step off the boat yourself and they will be stuck just as he was. Now mother let me get some sleep or I will eat up that boy hiding under the trough."

You can be sure he slept well for the rest of the night. The next morning the boy was given the three golden hairs and the three answers.

Going back the way he had come he came to the city with the fruit tree. He gave the king the answer and by the next morning there was fruit on the tree. The king was so pleased he was given six black horses and a bag of gold.

Next he came to the city with the stream and once more he gave the king the answer. As soon as the toad was taken out of the spring the stream began to flow. The king was so pleased he gave the boy six white horses and a bag of silver.

Finally the boy came to the river and the ferryman asked for his answer.

"I'll tell you on the other side," quipped the boy.

When they got to the other side and the boy and his horses were safely on the bank he told the ferryman to row his next passenger across the river, give the passenger the oar, step off himself and the passenger would be stuck just like he was.

The ferryman thanked him and the boy who continued on his journey.

As he approached his father-in-law's palace the king saw the horses and as he drew closer the bags of silver and gold.

"Where did you get those from?" asked the king, and the boy told him all about the stream that cured illnesses and the fruit that made you young again.

"I could use some water from that stream," thought the king, "and I could use some of that fruit."

So, the king set off on his journey and the first place he came to was the river and as far as I know that king has been rowing people from one side of the river to the other till this very day.

THE END

JOSÉ'S FIRST ADVENTURE

Once there was a chicken named José who had never been allowed out of the house alone.

But one day his mother decided he could go all by himself to his cousin's wedding on the other side of the town.

So she dressed him up in his best white feather suit and polished his beak, but before she let him out of door she made him promise not to talk to anybody and not to stop for anything on the way.

So off went José singing at the top of his voice, but unfortunately José had the worst voice in the *whole world*.

When he sang the insects put their fingers in their ears and the birds put their wings over their heads.

So as he was singing and walking down the road, he saw big, fat, juicy caterpillar crossing the road in front of him.

Now if there is one thing that chickens like it is big, fat, juicy caterpillars.

But José remembered what he had promised his mother and so he carried on down the road singing at the top of his voice.

The poor insects and birds covered their ears and heads so they couldn't hear the noise but José just kept on singing until, hopping across the road in front of him was a big, fat, juicy grasshopper.

Now if there is one thing that chickens like more than big, fat, juicy caterpillars it is big, fat, juicy grasshoppers. But José remembered what he had promised his mother so he carried on down the road singing at the top of his voice.

Suddenly José went quiet - much to the relief of all the birds and the insects.

Right in front of him was a bush full of beautiful big, fat, juicy, red berries.

Now if there is one thing that chickens like more than big, fat, juicy caterpillars and big, fat, juicy grasshoppers it is big, fat, juicy red berries and he thought to himself "Just one."

Well, it tasted *wonderful*, and because there was not one drop of berry juice on his beautiful white feather suit, he thought to himself "just another."

So José had another berry, and another and another!

By the time he had finished there was not one berry left on the bush and there was not one drop of berry juice on his suit.

José carried on towards the chapel singing at the top of his terrible voice.

Eventually even José got tired of his own voice and started to play another game: going cross eyed by looking at the end of beak.

To his horror he saw his beak was covered in berry juice!

So he went over to the grass and said "Grass, grass, wave in the wind and wipe the berry juice off my beak or I am going to be in big trouble."

But the grass answered "No way, José."

So he went to the sheep and said, "Sheep, sheep, eat grass, grass won't wave in the wind and wipe the berry juice off my beak and I am going to be in big trouble."

But the sheep answered "No way, José."

So he went to the wolf and said "Wolf, wolf, chase sheep, sheep won't eat grass, grass won't wave in the wind and wipe the berry juice off my beak and I am going to be in big trouble."

But the wolf answered "No way, José."

So he went to the dog and said "Dog, dog, bite wolf, wolf won't chase sheep, sheep won't eat grass, grass won't wave in the wind and wipe the berry juice off my beak and I am going to be in big trouble."

But the dog answered "No way, José."

So he went to the man and said, "Man, man, beat dog, dog won't bite wolf, wolf won't chase sheep, sheep won't eat grass, grass won't wave in the wind and wipe the berry juice off my beak and I am going to be in big trouble."

Now the man liked chickens so he said "OK, José."

So the man began to beat the dog.

The dog began to bite the wolf.

The wolf began to chase the sheep.

The sheep began to eat the grass.

The grass began to wave in the wind and wipe the berry juice off his beak and José was *not* in big trouble.

So José went running through the streets until he came to the chapel where his cousin's wedding was taking place. When he got to the entrance he threw the doors open and shouted, "I am here I can sing for you".

But the whole congregation turned and shouted "NO WAY, JOSÉ".

THE END

THE KNIGHTS OF THE LITTLE FISH

Way back in time when my hair was dark and my beard was ginger there lived a poor man and his wife.

They had next to nothing to eat. All they had was half a loaf of bread and that was dry and hard and had green mould growing on it. When that was gone there was nothing to eat at all.

Near them was a stream and there had been no fish in the stream for years but the man had a fishing rod and he thought it was worth a try, so he went down to the stream and cast his line.

When he pulled the line in there was a fish the colour of rainbows that had golden eyes. When he saw it he thought it was far too beautiful to eat and he was about to put it back in the water when the fish started talking to him.

"It's very kind of you," said the fish, "but completely unnecessary. I know you are very hungry so what you must do is this: Take me home, cook me, cut me into eight pieces, eat two pieces yourself, give two pieces to your wife to eat, bury two pieces in the ashes in the fire place and bury one piece on one side of the house and the last on the other."

Now I don't know about you but if a fish started talking to me I would do exactly as it said so the poor man went home and did everything the fish had told him.

He sat with his wife and ate the pieces of fish. After they had finished the meal they both felt full and satisfied.

"Indeed this is a magic fish," said the man.

But their luck didn't stop there. The next morning when they were cleaning out the fireplace, instead of two pieces of fish there were two bags of gold. So they bought the fields on either side of the stream.

Now, their luck didn't stop there either. For soon the wife had two fine sons and on the morning they were born one tree started growing one side of the house and another started growing on the other and nobody knew the names of the trees.

One morning the boys looked out of their window and saw hanging on the trees suits of armour, swords, helmets and shields and on the shields were painted pictures of little fish. Everything fitted the boys exactly and everyone called them the Knights of the Little Fish.

As if this wasn't enough, one morning they looked out at the paddock and there trotting round were two fine ponies exactly the right size for the boys.

The boys discussed their luck and decided they must have been given everything for a reason and they should take a journey to discover what the reason should be so they went to their mother and father and told them they were leaving. Their mother packed them up some food and drink, wished them good luck and waved goodbye to her children.

The two boys travelled together for years and years but as we all know if you are to have a great adventure you must go by yourself so one of the boys went to the east and the other the west. We will follow the one who went to the east.

He travelled for a long way and further still, till his throat was dry and his back was sore. Coming to a city he rode through the gates and saw that everyone was crying and tearing at their clothes.

He grabbed the nearest man and asked him what was wrong. He told him that every year they had to sacrifice a maiden to the dragon who was the son of the witch Albatross herself and if they didn't they would all be turned to stone. Not only that, but this year it was the turn of the princess and they didn't want the princess to be eaten by a dragon.

"Where is she?" asked the knight.

"Over there by the tree of ill omen," replied the man, and there was the tree of ill omen, all scorched and scarred by the dragon's breath and there was the princess.

"Ride away," she said "for there is not much time."

So he turned his pony and rode off.

"I know I said it but..." thought the princess. But before she could blink he was riding back and this time he had a mirror under his arm.

He put the mirror up against the tree, took a veil from the princess's head and covered the mirror with it and told her to wait until she could feel the dragon's breath upon her face and feel the ends of her hair burning. Only then was she to take the veil from the mirror and step smartly behind the tree.

I have met a lot of brave people in stories but none braver than this princess. She waited, and she waited, and she waited till she felt the breath upon her face and the ends of her hair burning and only then did she take the veil from the mirror and step smartly behind the tree. The dragon was looking straight into the mirror. It had never seen a mirror before and thought it was looking at an enemy. It breathed fire at the mirror, and the mirror breathed fire back. It stamped its foot, and the enemy stamped its foot back. The dragon got angrier, and angrier, and angrier. It broke the mirror into a thousand pieces so that now it was looking at a *thousand* enemies. It got even angrier and it started eating them.

Now, dragons are tough and this was the toughest dragon of them all but even he couldn't eat one thousand pieces of glass and there he was rolling around holding his middle when the knight stepped out from behind the tree and cut off the dragon's head.

The knight tied the dragon's head on a piece of rope and mounted his pony. The princess got on behind him and they rode off to the city with the dragon's head bouncing along behind them. When they got to the city everyone began clapping and cheering and everyone agreed that the princess should marry the Knight of the Little Fish, and the princess agreed she should marry the Knight of the Little Fish, and you can be sure the Knight of the Little Fish agreed she should marry the Knight of the Little Fish.

That night they were looking out of the princess's window and there in the distance was a great castle, a horrible castle. There were cobwebs running from the top of the tallest tower to the bottom of the deepest cellar with spiders the size of cats running up and down them and bats with blood covered teeth flying round the towers.

"Whose castle is that?" asked the knight.

"That is the castle of the witch Albatross herself," replied the princess. "Many have gone to visit but no-one has ever come back."

"*I* will," he thought, but he said nothing.

The next day he got on his pony and rode off to the castle. When he got to the orchard at the foot of the hill that the castle stood on the top of he tied up his pony and shouted "Is no-one inside alive?"

"No-one inside alive," came the echo.

"Is there no hospitality for a stranger?" meaning: "Can I have a cup of tea?"

"No hospitality for a stranger," came the echo.

Just then the most horrible, the most revolting, the most disgusting face you have ever seen in all of your life appeared at the window. It had a long hooked nose with a big wart on the end, a long hooked chin with three hairs sticking out, long fingers and long fingernails with snakes crawling around underneath them.

"My, what a handsome young man. Do step inside," screeched the witch.

He stepped inside.

"You are handsome, will you marry me?" squawked the witch.

"If it's alright with you, I'll just have a cup of tea and be on my way," replied the knight.

"First you must see the treasures in my castle," said the witch, as she led the boy past the tapestries with their moving figures and the statues that reached out and touched them as they passed.

When he thought he had seen everything he stammered "Forget the tea I think I'll be going now."

"First you must see the treasures in my cellar," whined the witch.

Well, you know there are times in your life when you are about to do something and you know if you do it you are going to get into lots and lots of trouble but you do it anyway - well it was like that with the boy.

He was halfway down the steps when he thought to himself, "I've done some stupid things in my life but nothing as stupid as following a witch down a set of steps with green slime falling off the walls on either side," and was about to tap the witch on the shoulder and tell her was going on his way when she stepped aside and he fell headfirst into the cellar.

"That will teach you not to marry me, oh slayer of my son the dragon," screamed the witch.

We will leave him there and see how his brother got on.

His brother had many adventures but he met no dragons. Eventually he came to the city and as he rode inside everyone began clapping and cheering. He thought they must have mistaken him for his brother and that if he kept quiet he might find out what had happened. As soon as they asked how he escaped from the witch Albatross he turned his pony and rode off towards the castle.

"That's strange," thought the princess, "he did not even stop to say hello."

When he came to the orchard he saw his brother's pony and tied his own pony to the same tree. He walked up the hill to the castle and banged on the big oak front door.

When the witch opened it she looked at him and screamed. She thought she was looking at the ghost of his brother. He took his sword and ran it through her middle.

"Now tell me where my brother is," ordered the knight.

"Only if you mend me," the witch replied.

"How can I mend you? I'm not a doctor."

"That is easy," was the witch's reply. "Go to the back of the castle, get some leaves stained with dragon's blood and some everlasting leaves and mix them in a tub and dip me in it," and that is exactly what he did. The witch was as good as new.

True to her word the witch took him to the cellar and showed him the body of his brother. When that too was dipped in the tub his brother was as good as new.

The brothers then went back down to the cellar and got the bodies of all the knights that had ever visited the castle and dipped them in the healing tub and they were all as good as new.

They returned to the cellar one last time and got all the bones of all of the maidens that had ever been eaten by the dragon and dipped *them* in the healing tub and all the maidens were as good as new.

The procession set off to the city while the witch stamped her foot, screamed and ran back into the castle slamming the door behind her. As soon as the door was closed the hillside opened and castle and witch were swallowed up. The hillside then closed sealing both castle and witch inside.

Back at the city there was a great celebration which lasted for seven days. At the end of seven days there was only one maiden left and she married the second knight. As you can guess the princess, the maiden and the two Knights of the Little Fish lived in that city happily for the rest of their lives.

THE END

THE RIBBON MAIDEN

Way back in time, in the middle of a village, in the middle of a forest, in the middle of China lived a young girl and she made the most beautiful ribbons you have ever seen in all of your life.

Everyone from that village sewed those ribbons onto their clothes and like anyone else with new clothes they would parade around the village showing them off.

But everyone had fine clothes with fine ribbons sewn on them so there was no-one to show them off *to*.

One day some of the villagers decided they should go to the city and naturally they wore their finest clothes decked with the finest of ribbons so when the people of the city saw them everyone admired them.

But in the middle of the city was a palace and in the middle of the palace was an emperor and he happened to be looking out of his window as the villagers passed by below.

He was dismayed to see that the villagers had better clothes than him, so he sent his servants to find out where they got them from.

When the servants came back with the news about the ribbon maiden he told them to stop standing around but to go and fetch her immediately.

Off went the servants, through the palace, through the city and through the forest till they came to the village where the ribbon maiden was making the most beautiful ribbons you have ever seen in all of your life.

"You girl," said the servants, "the emperor wants to see you."

"Well I do not particularly want to see the emperor," replied the ribbon maiden, hardly looking up from her sewing.

As we all know, it is very dangerous to turn down an invitation from the emperor and it would have been even more dangerous for the servants if they failed to obey the emperor's orders.

So without so much as an apology they picked her up, carried her through the forest, carried her through the city, carried her through the palace and threw her down at the emperor's feet.

"You girl," ordered the emperor pointing at her with his long bony finger, "you will make me the finest ribbons you have ever made in all of your life."

"Pardon me," she said, "you think you can send your servants to my village, insist I come to see you and when I refuse, have them pick me up, carry me through the forest, carry me through the city, carry me through the palace, throw me down at your feet and then you have the audacity to point at me with your long bony finger and tell me I have to make the finest ribbons I have ever made in all of my life. You do have to be joking."

Brave she might have been, but you cannot speak to emperors like that without terrible things happening to you.

It won't come as a surprise that the emperor was extremely angry, in fact he was furious, so he took her and locked her in a room and told her that she had seven days to sew him a live chicken. If not she would have her head chopped off.

The ribbon maiden was worried but she thought she would try. She took her needle and thread and she sewed, and she sewed, and she sewed, and at the end of seven days there was the most beautiful embroidered chicken but it was still an embroidered chicken, it was not alive.

She thought how lonely her body would be without a head on it and she cried, and she cried, and she cried, and a tear fell on the chicken and she bit her thumb and a drop of blood fell on the chicken. Suddenly there was a live chicken in the room.

In walked the emperor.

"There you are," she said. "That, if I am not mistaken, is a live chicken."

"You did not sew that," sneered the emperor. "Someone brought that in for you."

With that the chicken flapped its stumpy wings, jumped up, pecked the emperor in the face and flew out of the window.

"Right," said the emperor, "you have seven days to sew me a live peacock and I want to see every eye on every feather of its big fan tail. If not you know what happens: it's off with your head."

Once more the ribbon maiden took out her needle and thread and she sewed, and she sewed, and she sewed, and after seven days there was a magnificent embroidered peacock with every eye on every feather of its big fan tail. But it was still an embroidered peacock, it was not alive.

She thought how hard it would be for her to hold up her head without a body underneath it. So she cried, and she cried, and she cried, and a tear fell on the peacock and she bit her thumb and a drop of blood dropped on the peacock. Suddenly there was a live peacock in the room.

In walked the emperor.

"There you are," said the ribbon maiden. "If I am not mistaken that is a live peacock."

"You did not sew that, someone brought it in for you," replied the emperor.

With that the peacock jumped up, pecked the emperor in the face and flopped out the window. If ever you see a peacock trying to fly they flop.

"Right," said the emperor, "no more tricks, you have seven days to sew me a live dragon, if not, you will definitely lose your head."

She was even more worried this time but she sewed, and she sewed, and she sewed, and after seven days there was the most beautiful embroidered dragon. Like the ones on the back of silk dressing gowns but even better. But it was still an embroidered dragon, it was not alive.

She thought about her head rolling across the floor and she cried, and she cried, and she cried, and a tear fell on the dragon and she bit her thumb and a drop of blood fell on the dragon. Suddenly there was a live dragon in the room.

In walked the emperor.

But before he had a chance to speak the dragon breathed in and the dragon breathed out and we all know what happens when dragons breathe out. There was just a little pile of ashes where the emperor used to be.

"Where do you want to go?" asked the dragon.

"Back to my village," replied the girl.

"Get on my back," said the dragon.

The girl climbed on the dragon's back and they flew out of the window and twice round the palace. The dragon breathed in and the dragon breathed out and there was just a little pile of ashes where the palace used to be.

As they flew across the sky the ribbon maiden was so happy that she was making wonderful ribbons of all different colours and throwing them in the air and if you look up to the sky to this very if you are very lucky you will see a rainbow. When you do you will know it is where the ribbon maiden was making her way back home on the back of the dragon.

THE END

THE OLD WOMAN AND THE PIG

Long ago before anyone had thought of motor cars or computers there lived an old woman in a cottage.

All she had in the world in the way of money was a silver sixpence - a tiny coin worth two and a half pence.

In those days two and a half pence was a lot of money and when she lost it she searched the whole cottage for it and would not give up until it was back in her possession.

Eventually she found it under her pillow so she went to market and there she bought a pig.

She was walking home from the market, driving the pig in front of her, when she came to a stile. The pig refused to climb over it.

She went to the dog and said "Dog, dog, bite pig, piggy won't get over the stile and I shan't get home tonight."

The dog would not so she went to the stick and said, "Stick, stick, beat dog, dog won't bite pig, piggy won't get over the stile and I shan't get home tonight."

The stick would not so she went to the fire and said, "Fire, fire, burn stick, stick won't beat dog, dog won't bite pig, piggy won't get over the stile and I shan't get home tonight."

The fire would not so she went to the water and said, "Water, water, quench fire, fire won't burn stick, stick won't beat dog, dog won't bite pig, piggy won't get over the style and I shan't get home tonight."

The water would not so she went to the ox and said, "Ox, ox, drink water, water won't quench fire, fire won't burn stick, stick won't beat dog, dog won't bite pig, piggy won't get over the stile and I shan't get home tonight."

The ox would not so she went to the butcher and said, "Butcher, butcher, kill ox, ox won't drink water, water won't quench fire, fire won't burn stick, stick won't beat dog, dog won't bite pig, piggy won't get over the stile and I shan't get home tonight."

The butcher would not so she went to the rope and said, "Rope, rope, hang butcher, butcher won't kill ox, ox won't drink water, water won't quench fire, fire won't burn stick, stick won't beat dog, dog won't bite pig, piggy won't get over the stile and I shan't get home tonight."

The rope would not so she went to the rat and said, "Rat, rat, gnaw rope, rope won't hang butcher, butcher won't kill ox, ox won't drink water, water won't quench fire, fire won't burn stick, stick won't beat dog, dog won't bite pig, piggy won't get over the stile and I shan't get home tonight."

The rat would not so she went to the cat and said, "Cat, cat, catch rat, rat won't gnaw rope, rope won't hang butcher, butcher won't kill ox, ox won't drink water, water won't quench fire, fire won't burn stick, stick won't beat dog, dog won't bite pig, piggy won't get over the stile and I shan't get home tonight."

"Alright, alright, alright," said the cat. "Go to the cow over there and get me a saucer of milk and I'll catch your rat."

She went to the cow and said, "I haven't got time to explain but please give me a saucer of milk, if you would be so kind."

"Of course," replied the cow, "Go to that hay stack over there and get me an armful of hay and I will give you a saucer of milk."

Fortunately haystacks cannot speak, so she just grabbed an armful of hay and gave it to the cow.

The cow gave her a saucer of milk, and she gave the saucer of milk to the cat.

As soon as the cat had the saucer of milk it began to catch the rat, the rat began to gnaw the rope, the rope began to hang the butcher, the butcher began to kill the ox, the ox began to drink the water, the water began to put out the fire, the fire began to burn the stick, the stick began to beat the dog, the dog began to bite the pig, the piggy was so frightened it got straight over the stile and the old woman she got home that night.

THE END

THE GOLDEN NIGHTINGALE

A long time ago, longer than you and I could imagine, there lived a king with three sons.

One day the king was feeling particularly generous so he gave each of his sons a bag of gold to do with as they wished.

The three boys got together to discuss what they would do with the gold. The eldest thought he might throw a great party and invite all his friends.

The second thought he would buy a string of horses and stables to house them.

But the youngest thought it would be a wonderful thing if they were to get together and build a church in honour of their father so he would be remembered.

Reluctantly the two older brothers agreed, and they employed the finest architect in the land to design a great church with a tall tower and long stained glass windows.

Once the church was designed they got the finest stonemasons, builders and artists in the land to bring the plans to life.

When the church was complete they showed their father who was most impressed and thanked his sons profusely.

But just as the king was thinking to himself what wonderful sons he had, along came a little old man with a long white beard and long white hair that nearly touched the ground.

"Good morning your majesty," said the little old man. "What a very fine church with a very fine tower and very fine stained glass windows. It is a pity there is one thing missing."

"One thing missing!" exclaimed the king, "and what might that be?"

"A golden nightingale to sing on the roof," replied the little old man who shuffled off without another word.

The king called his boys to him. "It is a very fine church, with a very fine tower and very fine stained glass windows. But there is one thing missing," he said.

"And what might that be?" asked the oldest son, taken aback.

"A golden nightingale to sing on the roof," replied the king. "Whoever brings it to me will inherit my kingdom."

The three boys travelled together until they came to a place where the road split in three directions and one was 'The Road of No Returning', which the youngest brother took.

He travelled a long way till his feet were sore and his throat was dry and there he sat, made himself a fire by the side of the road and began to brew himself a pot of coffee.

He had not been there many minutes when along came a little old man with a long white beard and long white hair that nearly touched the ground.

The boy invited him to sit down and share a hot drink with him. The old man gratefully accepted the invitation and asked the boy where he was going.

"I am going to find a golden nightingale to sing on the roof of my father's church," replied the boy.

"You are going in the right direction," said the old man. "Continue down this road until you come to the castle of the forty ogres. There you will see an old woman in the garden hanging out the washing. Run up to her, throw your arms around her and say: 'Mother, Mother, Mother, save me from my forty brothers', and everything will begin to work out."

The next day the boy continued on his journey and did everything the old man had said. When the old woman heard what he had to say she brushed him down and turned him into a broom.

She put the broom in the corner of a huge dining room and waited for the forty ogres to return. When they came in she asked them what they would do if someone called her 'Mother'.

"Why, we would consider him our brother and be kind to him," said the ogres in unison.

As soon as they had spoken the old woman took the broom, tapped it twice upon the floor and it turned back into the boy. The ogres asked the boy his business and the boy told them that he was looking for a golden nightingale.

They pointed to a high shelf and there in a gilded cage was the golden nightingale.

"You may have it," they said, "if you go to the castle of the forty valiant youths and bring back the winged horse they stole from us."

So the boy immediately set off for the castle of the forty valiant youths. He walked for a long way and further still till his feet were sore and his throat was dry.

Once more he built a fire and brewed a pot of coffee, and along came the little old man with a long white beard and long white hair that nearly touched the ground.

The boy invited him to sit down and share the coffee. The old man thanked him, sat down and asked him where he was going.

When he told him he gave these instructions: "Go to the castle of the forty valiant youths, and go to the garden. There you will find an old woman hanging out the washing. Run up to her as you did before, throw your arms around her and say 'Mother, Mother, Mother, save me from my forty brothers' and things will continue to work out."

The boy did exactly as the old man said. This time he was given a good polish and he turned into apple.

The woman put the apple into a fruit bowl and waited for her children to return.

When they came in they all reached for the fruit bowl. The woman slapped each on the wrist and told them they would eat when she told them. In the meantime they were to tell her what they would do if someone was to call her 'Mother'.

"We would think he was our brother and be kind to him," they replied.

So their mother picked up the apple and gave it a polish. It turned back into the boy and the brothers were pleased they hadn't taken a bite out of it.

They asked him his business and when he told them they said he could have the winged horse if he brought them the Princess Five Times Fair.

And so the boy set off for the palace of the Princess Five Times Fair. When evening came he still had not reached his destination despite travelling so far that his feet were sore and his throat was dry.

Once more he lit a fire by the side of the road and began to brew a pot of coffee when who should come hobbling along the road but the little old man with a long white beard and long white hair that nearly touched the ground.

The boy invited him to rest for a while and share his coffee. As they drank the old man asked him where he was going and the boy told him.

"I have no advice this time," said the little old man, "but I do have this gift. It is a gun and whatever you aim at you will hit. It cannot miss."

The boy thanked the old man and set off down the road.

He had not gone far when he spied a vulture ahead of him pecking away at some poor creature that had met an unfortunate end. He put the gun to his shoulder and took aim. To his surprise the vulture began to beg for its life.

"Spare me, spare me, spare me and when you are in trouble I will help you. Here, take a feather from my tail and when you have need of me all you have to do is call and I will be with you before you can blink."

So the boy took a feather from the vulture's tail, put it in his bag and carried on down the road until he came to a stream. There, swimming just below the surface of the water was a fine salmon. Once more he put the gun to his shoulder only to hear the salmon beg for its life too.

"Spare me, spare me, spare me and when you are in trouble I will help you. Here, take a scale from my back and when you have need of me call and I will be there before you have time to draw breath."

So the boy bent down, took a scale from the salmon's back, popped it in his bag and carried on down the road, when, what did he see in front of him but a fox. For the third time he shouldered his gun but as you can guess, the fox also begged for its life.

"Spare me, spare me, spare me and when you are in trouble I will help you. Here, take a hair from my bushy tail and when you have need of me call and I will be by your side before the words are out of your mouth."

So the boy plucked a hair from the fox's tail, put it in his bag and continued his journey until he came to the city of the Princess Five Times Fair.

When he let it be known that he was looking for the princess he was taken to her father, the king. He said he would be pleased to be rid of her but whoever took her would have to play hide and seek with her and hide for three hours without being found.

Being a generous man in his own eyes he allowed each person three turns, but if the third failed then their head would be chopped off and put on a spike on the city walls.

The king pointed to the heads of all the men who had failed in the past, but the boy was not to be put off.

"Very well," said the king, "on your own head be it."

And so the princess was blindfolded and began to count. The boy ran off, pulled out the vulture's feather and called for its help. Before he could blink the vulture was by his side asking what the boy wanted done.

"Quick," said the boy, "let me climb on your back so you can fly me to the sky and hide me behind a cloud."

The vulture did as the boy asked.

"Forty eight, forty nine, fifty, coming to get you ready or not!" called the princess.

She looked to the left, to the right, up and down and around and around but she could not find the boy anywhere. With only a few minutes left, she looked to the sky and saw the boy's heel sticking out from behind a cloud.

"I can see you!" shouted the princess.

"Two goes left, then it is off with your head," said the king, rubbing his hands together in anticipation.

The princess put on the blindfold and started counting again. This time the boy went down by the sea and called the salmon. Before he could draw breath there was the fish asking him what he wanted.

"Hurry," said the boy, "hide me at the bottom of the sea."

He climbed on the salmon's back and they swam to the bottom of the sea where the boy hid behind a rock.

"Forty eight, forty nine, fifty, coming to get you ready or not!" called the princess.

She looked here and she looked there. She looked up and she looked down but the boy was nowhere to be found. Then, with only a few seconds remaining, she spied his ear sticking out from behind a rock at the bottom of the sea.

"I can see you!" screamed the princess.

"One go left, then your head will be mine and stuck on a spike on the city wall," said the king, hardly able to contain himself.

For one last time the princess put on the blindfold and began counting. This time the boy took the fox's hair and called for its help. Before the words were out of his mouth the fox was by his side asking what the boy wanted done.

"There is no time to waste," said the boy, "hide me in the middle of the Earth."

The boy got on the fox's back and together they went to the middle of the Earth where the fox left the boy to wait.

"Forty eight, forty nine, fifty coming to get you ready or not!" called the princess, but this time when she took off the blindfold and opened her eyes there was the fox right in front of her dancing a jig.

She had never seen anything like it before in her life. She forgot all about looking for the boy. The fox danced, and he danced, and he danced, and when he had finished dancing he began to swing through the trees from one branch to another, and when he had finished with that he began to do summersaults and cartwheels across the lawn.

He kept this up for three hours and never once during that time did the princess take her eyes off the fox.

When the three hours were up the fox went back down to the centre of the earth and fetched up the boy.

The king could do nothing but let the boy go and take his daughter with him.

The princess was quite relieved. She had become more than a little fed up with her father cutting off the heads of all the young men who came to visit her.

Her relief was not to last long. The boy apologised to her before explaining that he was going to have to swap her for a winged horse at the castle off the forty valiant youths.

"I do however, have a plan," he said. "Trust me. When I swap you for the horse stand close to me. As I take-off, wave goodbye and I will grab your hand and swing you onto the back of the horse and we will fly off together."

The princess was not at all sure but she did as the boy ordered and much to her surprise everything went according to plan.

As they flew towards the castle of the forty ogres, he explained that their troubles were not over yet. Although he was supposed to swap the winged horse for the golden nightingale he knew that as soon as the ogres saw the princess they would want her instead.

"Do not worry," he said. "Do the same as we did at the castle of the forty valiant youths and all will be well. It worked once and it will work again."

Again the princess was not at all sure but she did as the boy suggested. This time when the boy flew off he had the winged horse, the Princes Five Times Fair *and* the golden nightingale and the ogres had nothing but their frustration.

However, the boy had not anticipated the jealousy of his brothers and when he got back to the place where the road had split into three directions his brothers were waiting.

They took him, threw him into a pit and got on the back off the winged horse. But the beast refused to fly so the brothers had to walk, dragging the princess along behind them.

When they got back to the city the eldest brother gave the nightingale to his father who put it on the roof of the church. The two brothers had agreed to split the inheritance but it was the elder who was to marry the princess.

On the day of the wedding the nightingale refused to sing and the princess refused to smile but all the same it seemed that nothing could stop the ceremony.

The service was half-way through and the priest was about to ask if each would take the other's hand in marriage when the winged horse burst through the door with the youngest son on its back. As soon as the princess saw the boy she began to smile, while on the roof the golden nightingale burst into song. The old king realised what a mistake he had made and gave everything to his youngest son.

The two older brothers were banished from that land for ever and they were lucky enough not to have been put into barrels of nails and dropped into the sea. In fact they would have been had not their younger brother pleaded for their lives.

As for the princess, she married the youngest son and together they lived happily and ruled justly for the rest of their days.

THE END

CUT ME DOWN TO SIZE

There was once a merchant leading an ox down a rough road, and on the back of the ox was a huge sack of peas.

As the ox swayed from side to side the sack began to fall to the ground. Realising the sack was too heavy for him to lift by himself the merchant looked round for some help, but the only living creature in sight was a mouse.

"Excuse me mouse," said the merchant. "Would you mind helping me to put this sack of peas back onto the ox?"

"Not at all," replied the mouse, not in the least surprised to hear a talking merchant.

So between them they wrestled the sack back onto the ox, and when they had finished, the merchant was so pleased that he gave the mouse one pea.

One pea had already fallen out onto the road, so the mouse now had *two* peas, and because he did not trust the merchant in the first place he had already taken one so he had *three* peas.

The mouse planted the peas in a row outside his hole and said to the peas: "Unless there are three fine green shoots by the morning I'll cut you up and feed you to the ox."

And you can be sure that when he woke up there were three fine, green shoots growing outside his hole.

The next day he said to the shoots: "Unless there are three fine flowers by the morning, I'll cut you up and feed you to the ox."

And you can be sure that when he woke up there were three fine flowers growing outside his hole.

On the third day he said to the flowers: "Unless there are three fine pods with fat peas inside by tomorrow morning I'll cut you up and feed you to the ox."

And you can be sure when he woke up there were three fine pods with fat peas inside.

So he ate, and he ate, and he ate. Each day he ate more, and more, and more and his waist got larger, and larger, and larger.

Now, if you were a mouse and you had a large waist everyone would think you were really good looking.

So one day he bumped into a female mouse and she wanted to know how he got such a wonderfully large waist.

So he took her back home and they both sat outside his hole and ate lots and lots of peas.

When they'd had enough she ran down the mouse hole.

He tried to run down behind her but he got stuck halfway down.

So the mouse went the carpenter and said, "Carpenter, carpenter, cut me down to size so I can get down my hole."

But the carpenter replied, "Do you mind? I have all this furniture to finish by tomorrow morning, I haven't got time to deal with a mouse. Go away."

So the mouse went to the king and said, "King, king, tell carpenter to cut me down to size so I can get down my hole."

But the king replied, "Do you mind? I've got a whole country here, I haven't got time to deal with a mouse. Go away."

So the mouse went to the queen and said, "Queen, queen, leave king, king won't tell carpenter to cut me down to size so I can get down my hole."

But the Queen replied, "Do you mind? I am not going to leave the king for a mouse! Go away."

So the mouse went to the snake and said, "Snake, snake, bite queen, queen won't leave king, king won't tell carpenter to cut me down to size so I can get down my hole."

But the snake replied, "Do you mind? This is the first hot day for months. I just want to lay here basking in the sun. Go away."

So the mouse went to the stick and said, "Stick, stick, beat snake, snake won't bite queen, queen won't leave king, king won't tell carpenter to cut me down to size so I can get down my hole."

But the stick replied, "Do you mind? I have spent all day beating a thief; I haven't got any energy left. Go away."

So the mouse went to the furnace and said, "Furnace, furnace, burn stick, stick won't beat snake, snake won't bite queen, queen won't leave king, king won't tell carpenter to cut me down to size so I can get down my hole."

But the furnace replied, "Do you mind? I'm cooking the king's dinner here, I haven't got time to deal with a mouse. Go away."

So the mouse went to the ocean and said, "Ocean, ocean, put out furnace, furnace won't burn stick, stick won't beat snake, snake won't bite queen, queen won't leave king, king won't tell carpenter to cut me down to size, so I can get down my hole."

But the ocean replied, "Do you mind? The tide is high, the fish are jumping and the sun is in the sky, I haven't got time to deal with a mouse. Go away."

So the mouse went to the elephant and said, "Elephant, elephant drink ocean, ocean won't put out furnace, furnace won't burn stick, stick won't beat snake, snake won't bite queen, queen won't leave king, king won't tell carpenter to cut me down to size so I can get down my hole."

But the elephant replied, "Do you mind? I have just drunk a lake, I haven't got room for an ocean. Go away."

So the mouse went to the vine and said, "Vine, vine, strangle elephant, elephant won't drink ocean, ocean won't put out furnace, furnace won't burn stick, stick won't beat snake, snake won't bite queen, queen won't leave king, king won't tell carpenter to cut me down to size so I can get down my hole."

But the vine replied, "Do you mind? I am stuck to this tree, I couldn't help you even if I wanted to. Go away."

So the mouse went to the scythe and said, "Scythe, scythe cut down vine, vine won't strangle elephant, elephant won't drink ocean, ocean won't put out furnace, furnace won't burn stick, stick won't beat snake, snake won't bite queen, queen won't leave king, king won't tell carpenter to cut me down to size so I can get down my hole."

Fortunately for your breath and everybody's patience the scythe said, "OK."

So the scythe began to cut down the vine, the vine began to strangle the elephant, the elephant began to drink the ocean, the ocean began to put out the furnace, the furnace began to burn the stick, the stick began to beat the snake, the snake began to bite the queen, the queen began to leave the king, so the king told the carpenter to cut the mouse down to size and the mouse got down its hole.

THE END

ABOUT JOHN ROW

John tells stories in schools and literature festivals around the world. A veteran performer at village and community days, John collects his own audiences and holds them spellbound with his stories. Listeners return year after year to hear him perform.

He encourages participation when telling, and encourages listeners to repeat the stories to other people.

He tells stories at Cambridge Children's Festival, Glastonbury Festival, Guilfest, Cropready, Cambridge Folk Festival, Keerville Folk Festival (Texas), George West Storyfest (Texas), Austin International Poetry Festival, Eastern Haze and Strawberry Fair, as well as numerous village, town and city open air events.

He was the first *Storyteller in Residence* in a British prison and was *Writer in Residence* at 'H.M.P. Highpoint' from 2004-2008. Currently he is *Writer in Residence* at HMP Blundeston.

He has created characters for recycling and public information road shows and has scripted films and plays in prisons.

For more information on John Row, or to arrange a visit to a school, festival, or other special event visit:

www.authorsabroad.com